Per Luca, con amore —D.M.

For Isabel —B.S.

When we plant trees, we plant the seeds of peace and seeds of hope.

—Dr. Wangari Maathai, 2004 Nobel Peace Prize laureate

Visit us on the Web! randomhousekids.com

Educators and librarians, for a variety of teaching tools, visit us at RHTeachersLibrarians.com

The Library of Congress has cataloged the hardcover edition of this work as follows:
Muldrow, Diane.
We planted a tree / by Diane Muldrow ; illustrated by Bob Staake.
p. cm.
"A Golden book."
Summary: Simple text reveals the benefits of planting a single tree, both to those who see it grow and to the world as a whole.
ISBN 978-0-375-86432-2 (hardcover) – ISBN 978-0-375-96432-9 (hardcover library binding) – ISBN 978-0-375-98304-7 (ebook)
[1. Trees–Fiction. 2. Ecology–Fiction.] I. Staake, Bob, ill. II. Title.
PZ7.M8894We 2010
[E]–dc22 2009000394

ISBN 978-0-553-53903-5 (pbk.)

MANUFACTURED IN CHINA
10 9 8 7 6
First Dragonfly Books Edition

Random House Children's Books supports the First Amendment and celebrates the right to read.

We Planted a Tree

BY DIANE MULDROW
ILLUSTRATED BY BOB STAAKE

Dragonfly Books  New York

We planted a tree.

We planted a tree and it grew up . . .

We planted a tree and it grew up,
While it reached for the sky and the sun.

The sunshine went into the leaves
And brought food to the tree,
And the tree grew up.

Fat little buds appeared on the branches.

The sunshine went into the buds,
And soon they burst open.

Everywhere it was pink,
And we were dizzy
With springtime.

The sun kept shining.
The pink blossoms dropped off,
But soon there were green leaves.
Green, green, shiny leaves,
Which had food inside for the tree.

Green, green, shiny leaves,
Which cooled us,
Which kept the earth cool.

We planted a tree and it grew up,
And gave us a shady place.

The tree's leaves helped clean the air,
And we breathed better.

The tree fed us—
Apples and oranges

And lemons

And sap for our syrup.

We planted a tree, and it grew up.

The tree kept the soil from blowing away—
Now rainwater could stay in the earth.

The soil became healthier
Because the tree was there,
So we planted.

We planted butternut squash and beans,
Corn and onions and cabbage,
In the healthy soil, the rich, dark dirt.

We could grow our own food,
And we ate better.

We planted a tree and it grew up,

And it dropped acorns
That fed the squirrels in winter.
And birds came,
And other animals came, too,
To live with the tree.

We planted a tree,
And that one tree
Made the world better.

We planted a tree,

And that one tree
Helped heal the earth.

We planted a tree and it grew up,

And so did we.